Henry Builds a Cabin

✧ *For my father* ✧

www.houghtonmifflinbooks.com

The text of this book is set in Bodoni Book.
The illustrations are colored pencil and paint on paper.

Library of Congress Cataloging-in-Publication Data

Johnson, D. B. (Donald B.), 1944–
Henry builds a cabin / by D. B. Johnson.
p. cm.
Summary: Young Henry Thoreau appears frugal to his friends as he sets
about building a cabin. Includes biographical information about Thoreau.
ISBN 0-618-13201-5
1. Thoreau, Henry David, 1817–1862—Juvenile Fiction. [1. Thoreau, Henry
David, 1817–1862—Fiction. 2. Buildings—Fiction. 3. Saving and
investment—Fiction.] I. Title.
PZ7.J6316355 Hd 2002
[Fic]—dc21   2001039257

Manufactured in the United States of America
WOZ 10 9 8 7 6 5 4 3 2

7-16-02

⇥ Henry Builds a Cabin ⇤

D. B. Johnson

HOUGHTON MIFFLIN COMPANY
BOSTON

One spring day Henry decided to build a cabin.

He borrowed an ax and cut down twelve trees.

Henry cut the logs into square beams.

He notched the bottom beams to fit into corner posts. The corner posts fit into ceiling beams. And the ceiling beams fit into roof beams.

In April his friend Emerson helped raise the beams.
The work made him hungry.

"Henry," he said, "your cabin looks too small to eat in!"
"It's bigger than it looks," said Henry.

And he led his friend to a bean patch he had planted behind the cabin.

"When it's finished, this will be my dining room."

In May Henry bought an old shed and took it apart.

He nailed the boards on the floor, the roof, and the walls of his cabin.

Henry was nailing the last board when his friend Alcott arrived.

"Henry," he said, "your cabin looks too dark to read in!"
"It's brighter than it looks," said Henry.

And he led his friend to a sunny spot beside the cabin.

"When it's finished, this will be my library."

In June Henry put a door in front.
Then he put two used windows in the side walls.

He bought old shingles for the roof and walls.

Henry was nailing the last shingle when Miss Lydia peeked in the window.

"Henry," she said, "your cabin looks too small to dance in!"
"It's bigger than it looks," said Henry.

And he led her to the front of the cabin, where a path curved down to the pond.

"When it's finished, this will be the ballroom with a grand stairway."

On the Fourth of July Henry moved into his cabin.

Tongs
Kettle
Skillet
Frying Pan
3 Knives+Forks
3 Plates
Dipper
1 Cup 1 Spoon
Molasses Jug
Oil Jug

Bed
Table 3 Chairs
Desk
Mirror
Books
Wash Bowl

He ate beans in his dining room.

He read in his library.

And he danced down the grand stairway to the pond.

When it started to rain, Henry ran back to his cabin.

"It's bigger than it looks," he said.
"This is just the room I wear when it's raining!"

⇥ About Henry's Cabin ⇤

Henry David Thoreau was a real person who lived in Concord, Massachusetts, more than 150 years ago. In the woods beside Walden Pond he built a cabin. It was 10 feet wide and 15 feet long, just big enough for his bed, a writing desk, a table, and three chairs. Henry wanted his cabin to be small so it wouldn't cost much money. He bought used windows and old boards and bricks that cost less than new ones. And he built the cabin himself (with the help of his friends) instead of paying someone to build it for him. Altogether, the cabin cost only $28.12 ½.

Henry moved into his cabin on July 4, 1845. Before the snow came he built a fireplace and chimney and plastered the walls to keep out the cold air. He lived at the pond for two years.

The people of Concord wondered: Why would Henry move to the woods away from town? Henry wanted a quiet place to write a book about what he loved, the wild outdoors. He kept a journal to tell about what he saw in the woods and the pond: how plants and animals changed with the seasons, when flowers bloomed and berries ripened. And his life in the woods showed people how to live happily without spending all their time earning money. The book Henry wrote about this time is called *Walden*. In it he says:

"Most men appear never to have considered what a house is, and are actually though needlessly poor all their lives because they think they must have such a one as their neighbors have."

Boards	*$8.03 ½*
Used shingles	*4.00*
Laths	*1.25*
Two second-hand windows	*2.43*
One thousand old bricks	*4.00*
Two casks of Lime*	*2.40*
Hair*	*0.31*
Mantle-tree iron	*0.15*
Nails	*3.90*
Hinges and screws	*0.14*
Latch	*0.10*
Chalk	*0.01*
Transportation	*1.40*
	$28.12 ½

* lime and hair were used to make plaster